THIS BOOK BELONGS TO

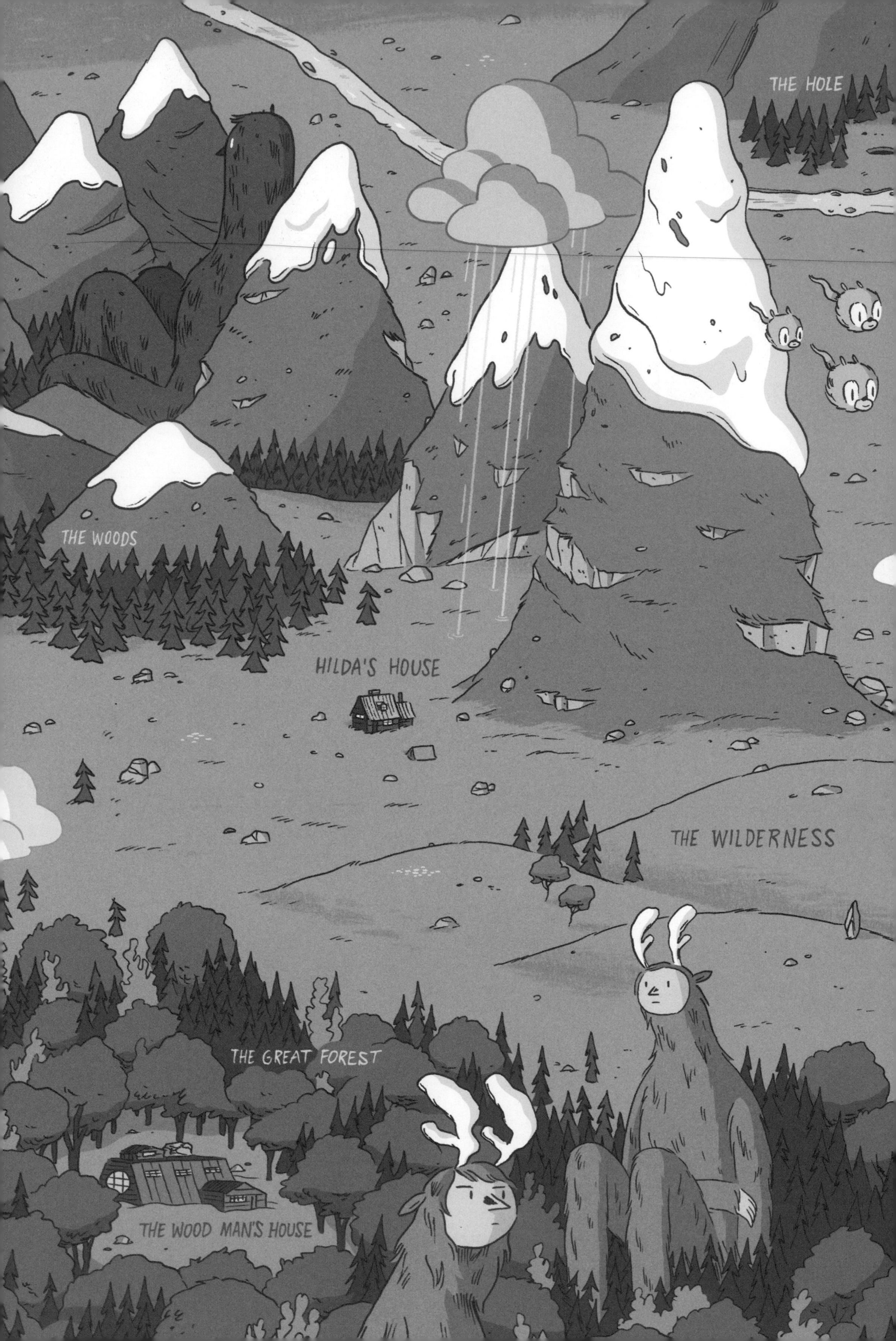
THE HOLE
THE WOODS
HILDA'S HOUSE
THE WILDERNESS
THE GREAT FOREST
THE WOOD MAN'S HOUSE

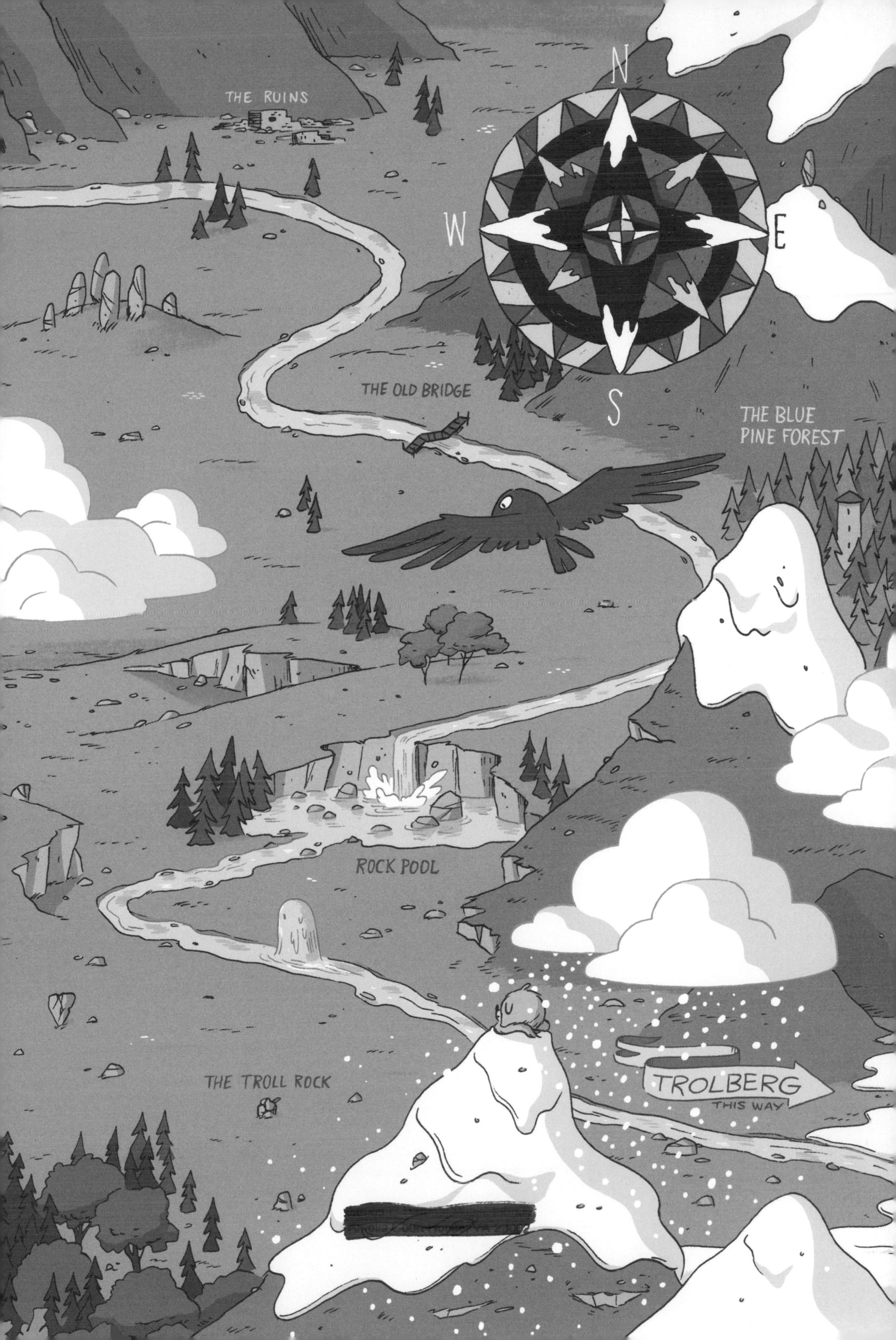
N
W
E
S
THE RUINS
THE OLD BRIDGE
THE BLUE PINE FOREST
ROCK POOL
THE TROLL ROCK
TROLBERG
THIS WAY
[redacted]

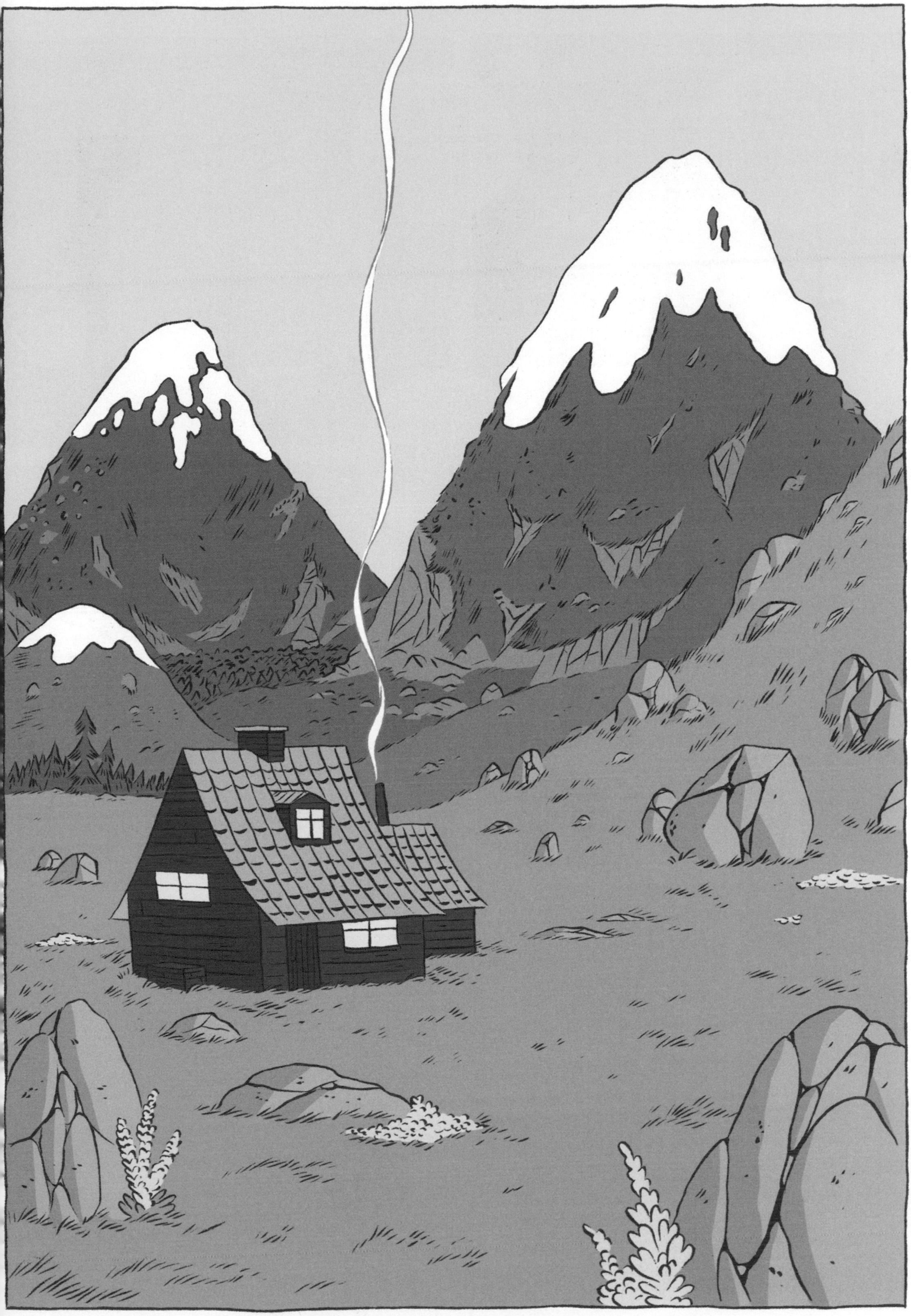

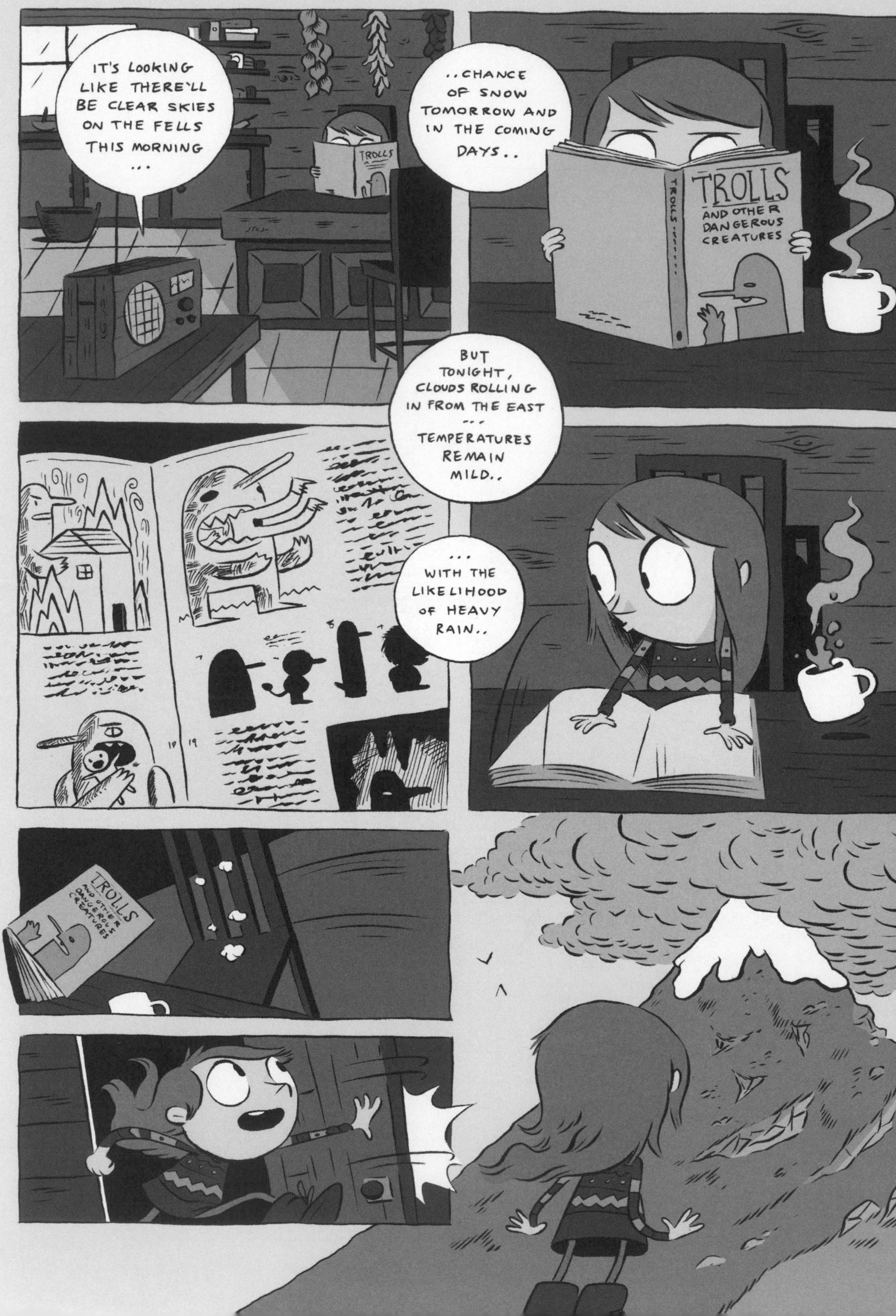

IT'S LOOKING LIKE THERE'LL BE CLEAR SKIES ON THE FELLS THIS MORNING ...
TROLLS
..CHANCE OF SNOW TOMORROW AND IN THE COMING DAYS..
TROLLS AND OTHER DANGEROUS CREATURES
BUT TONIGHT, CLOUDS ROLLING IN FROM THE EAST --- TEMPERATURES REMAIN MILD..
... WITH THE LIKELIHOOD OF HEAVY RAIN..
TROLLS AND OTHER DANGEROUS CREATURES

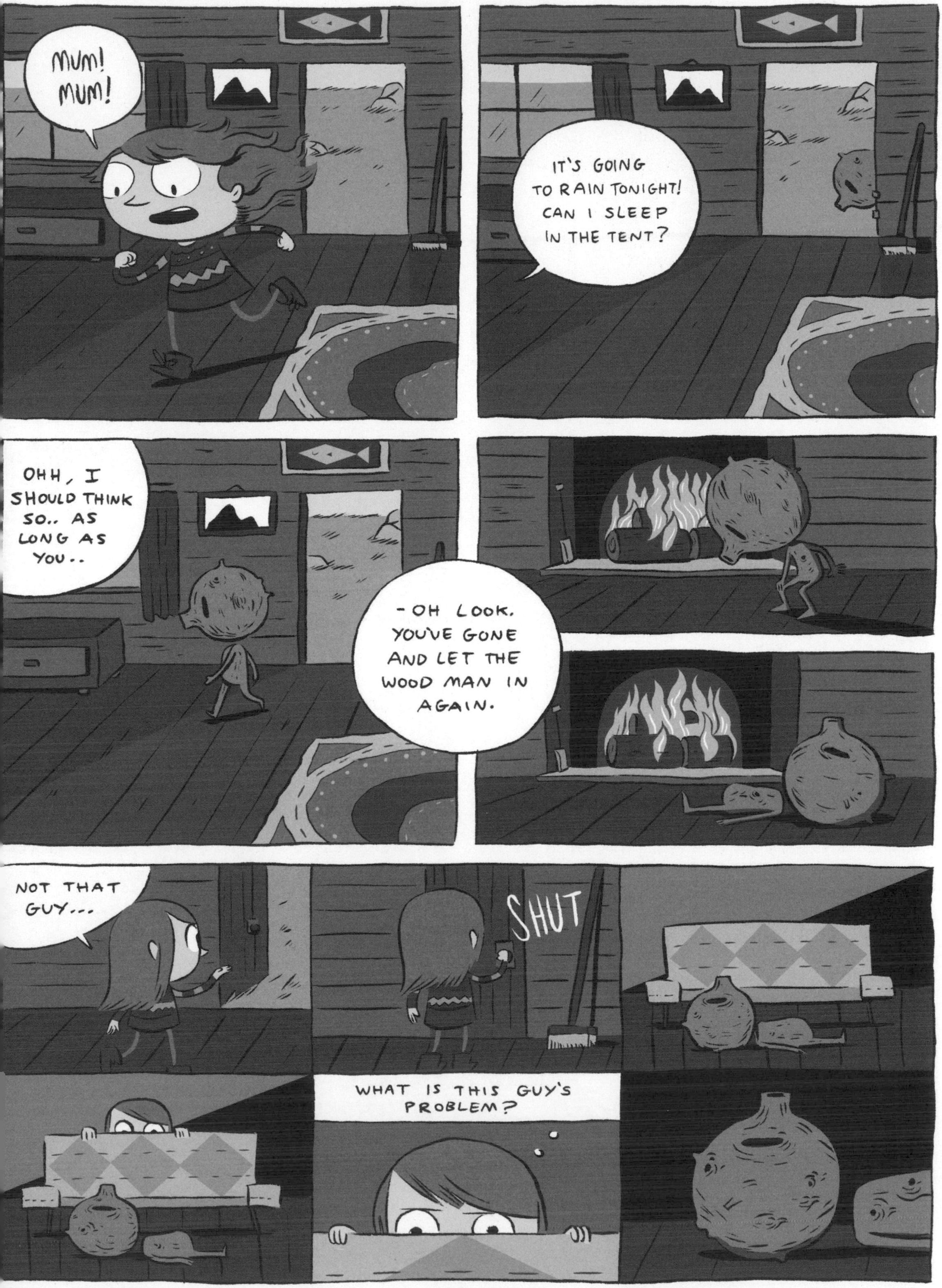
MUM! MUM!
IT'S GOING TO RAIN TONIGHT! CAN I SLEEP IN THE TENT?
OHH, I SHOULD THINK SO.. AS LONG AS YOU..
-OH LOOK. YOU'VE GONE AND LET THE WOOD MAN IN AGAIN.
NOT THAT GUY...
SHUT
WHAT IS THIS GUY'S PROBLEM?

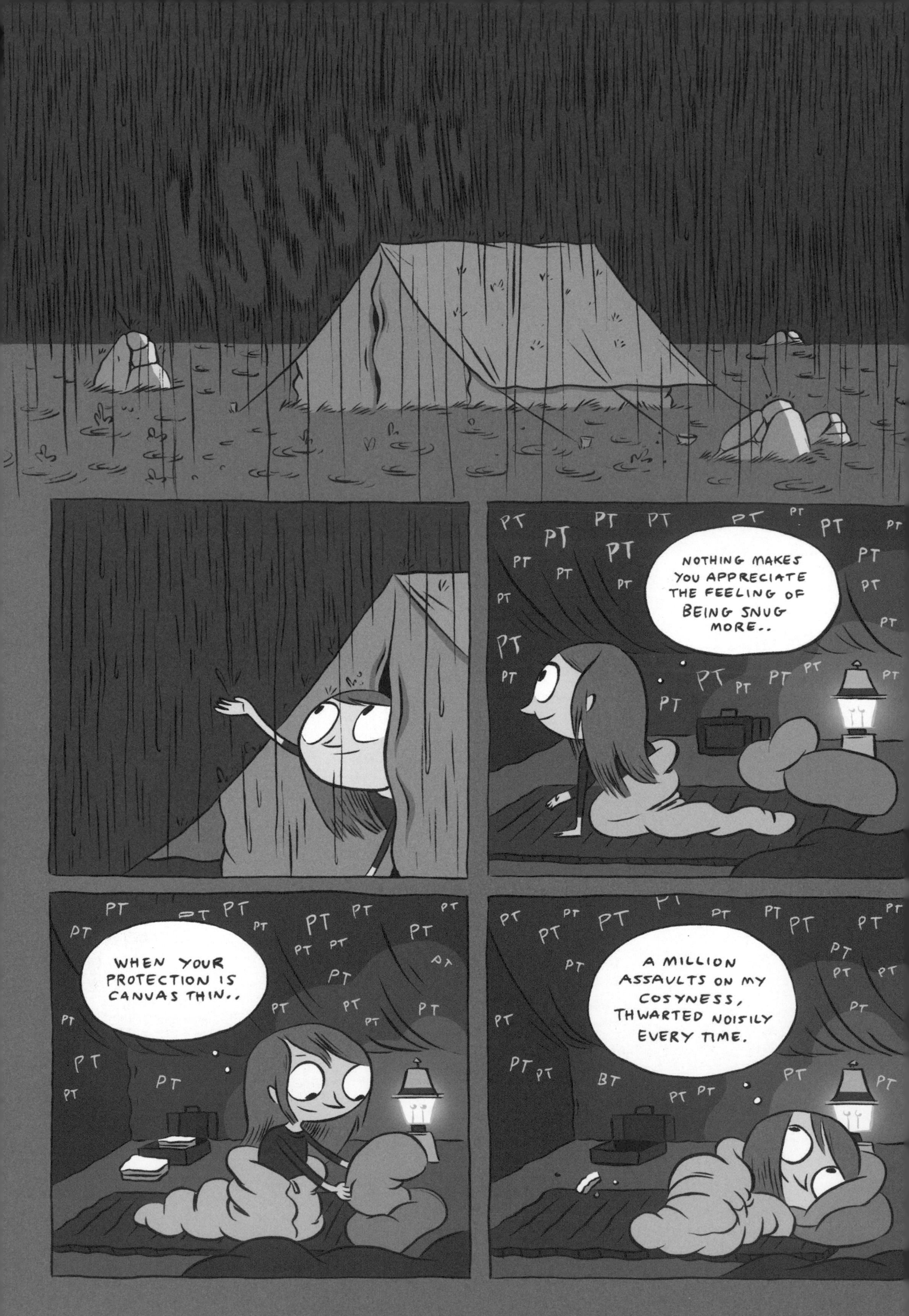
NOTHING MAKES YOU APPRECIATE THE FEELING OF BEING SNUG MORE..
WHEN YOUR PROTECTION IS CANVAS THIN..
A MILLION ASSAULTS ON MY COSYNESS, THWARTED NOISILY EVERY TIME.

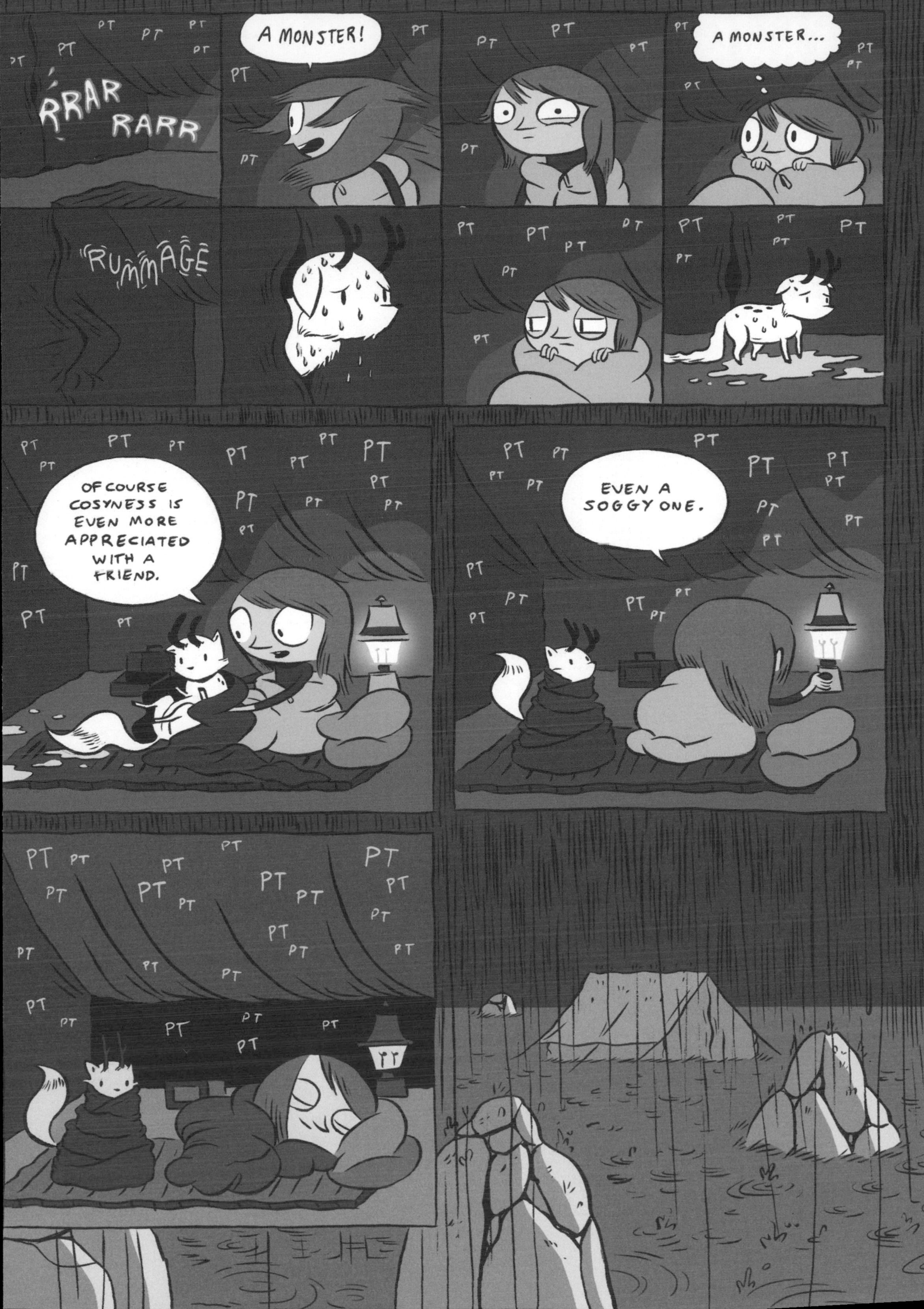
PT PT PT PT PT PT
RRAR RARR
A MONSTER!
PT PT PT
A MONSTER...
RUMMAGE
OF COURSE COSYNESS IS EVEN MORE APPRECIATED WITH A FRIEND.
EVEN A SOGGY ONE.

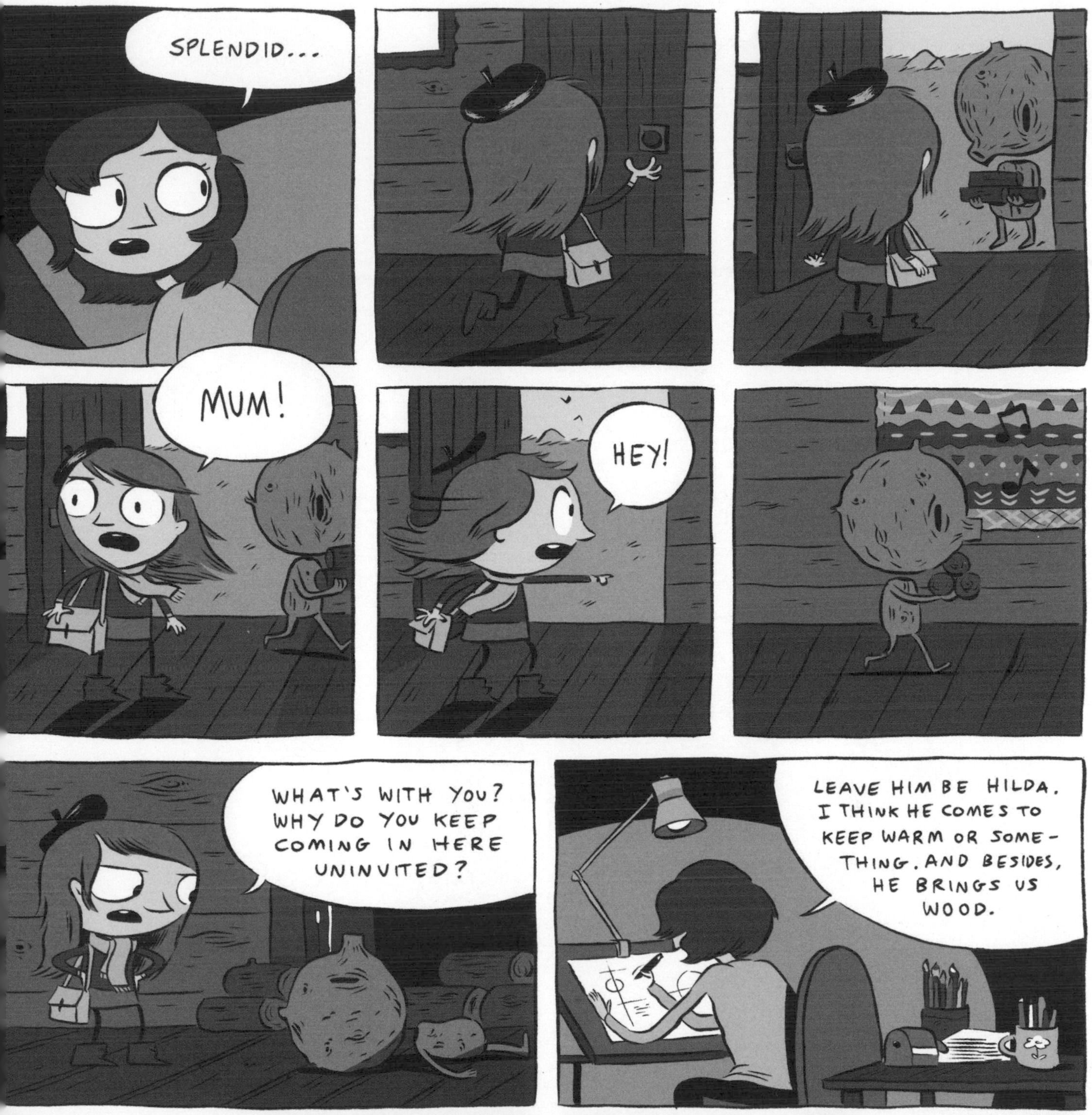
SPLENDID...
MUM!
HEY!
WHAT'S WITH YOU? WHY DO YOU KEEP COMING IN HERE UNINVITED?
LEAVE HIM BE HILDA. I THINK HE COMES TO KEEP WARM OR SOME-THING. AND BESIDES, HE BRINGS US WOOD.
WELL I STILL THINK HE'S VERY RUDE. AND A WEIRDO TOO..
..DON'T YOU HAVE YOUR OWN HOUSE?

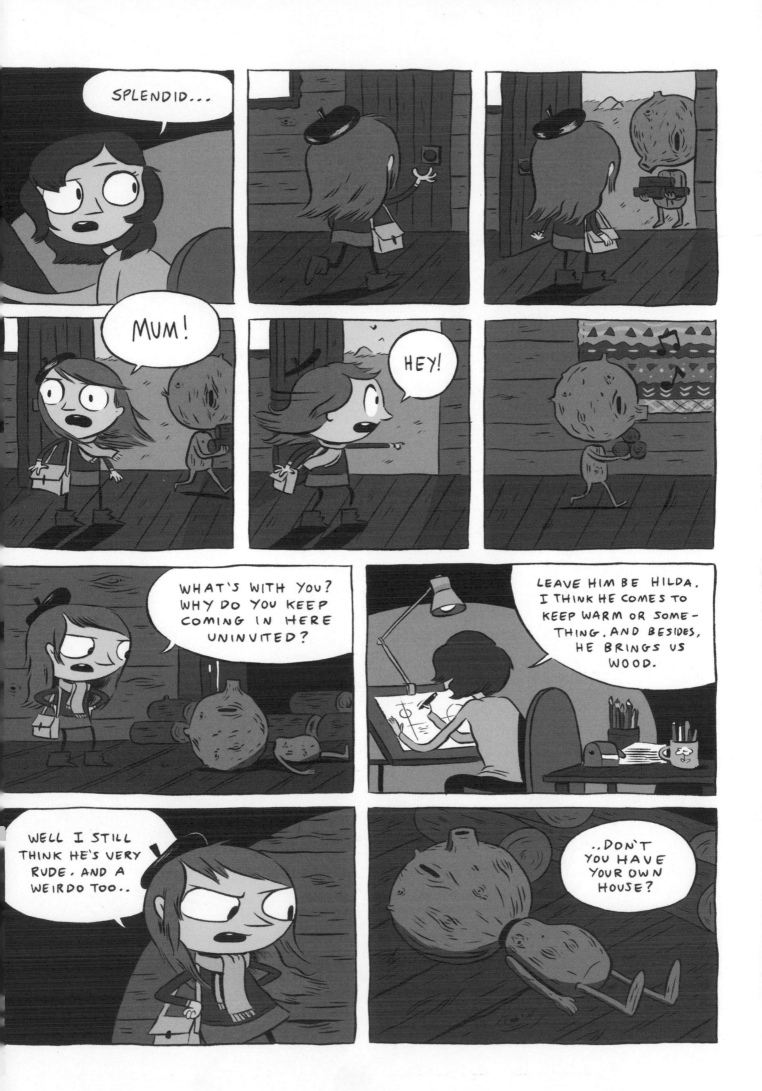

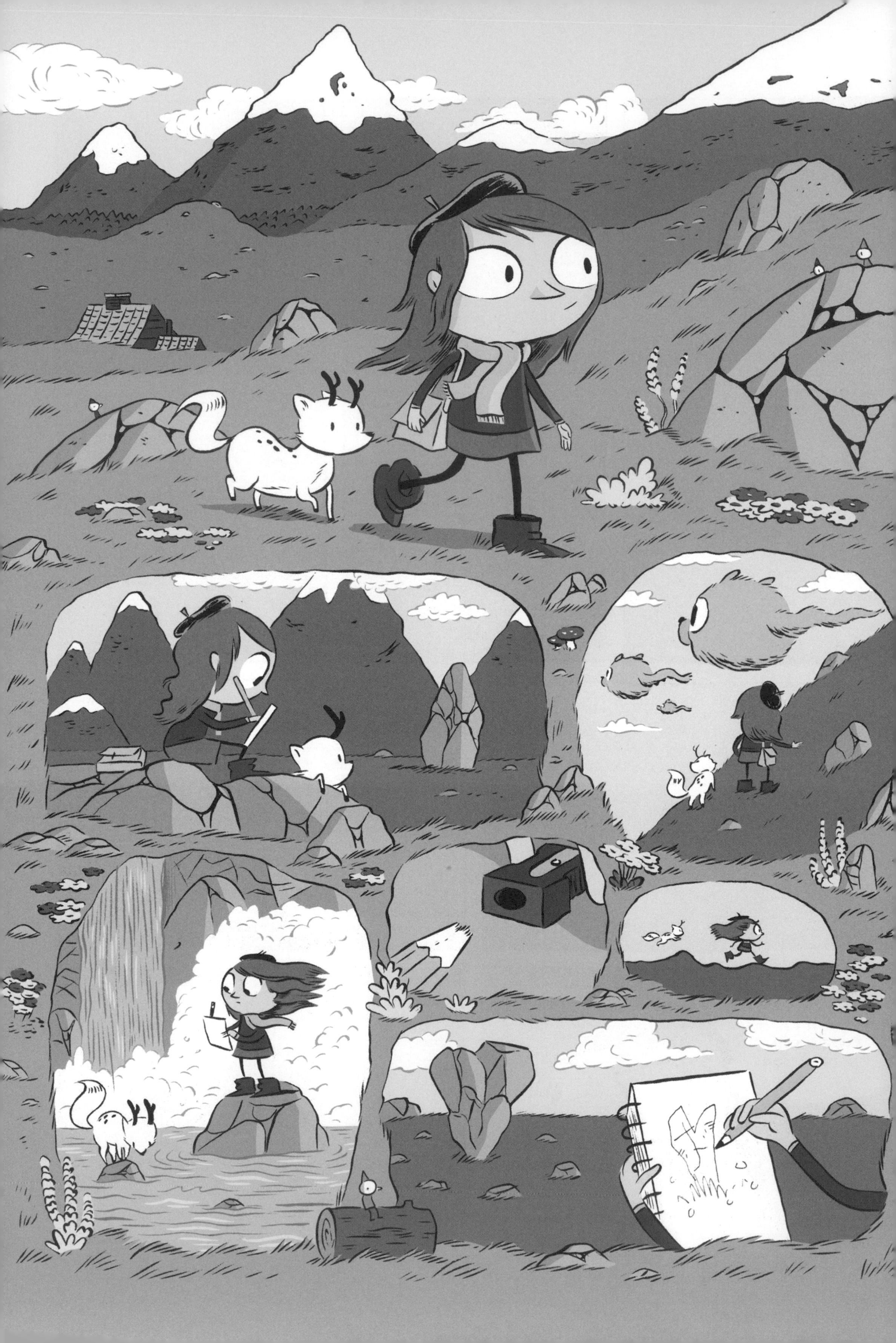

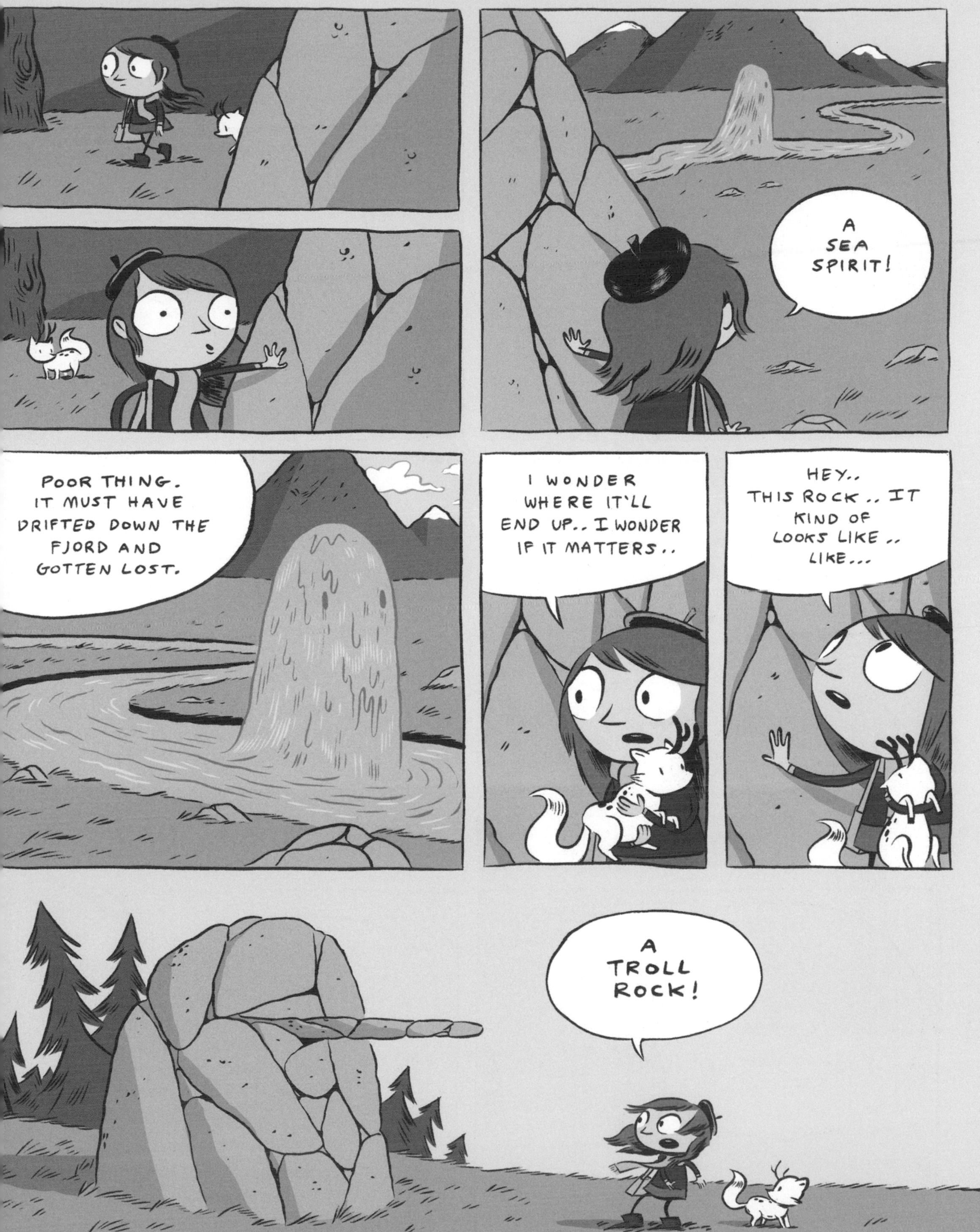
A SEA SPIRIT!
POOR THING. IT MUST HAVE DRIFTED DOWN THE FJORD AND GOTTEN LOST.
I WONDER WHERE IT'LL END UP.. I WONDER IF IT MATTERS..
HEY.. THIS ROCK .. IT KIND OF LOOKS LIKE .. LIKE...
A TROLL ROCK!

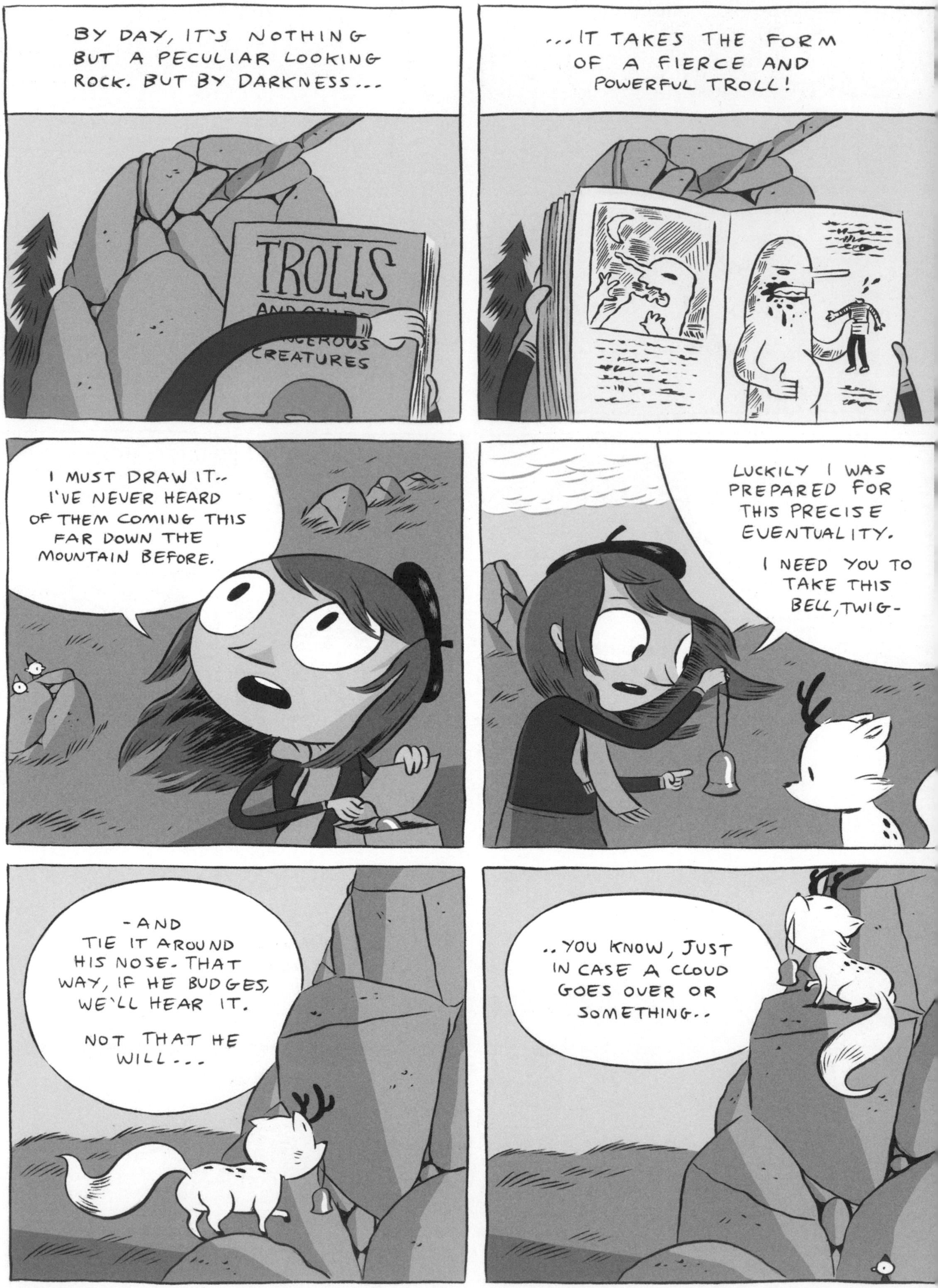
BY DAY, IT'S NOTHING BUT A PECULIAR LOOKING ROCK. BUT BY DARKNESS...
TROLLS
CREATURES
...IT TAKES THE FORM OF A FIERCE AND POWERFUL TROLL!
I MUST DRAW IT.. I'VE NEVER HEARD OF THEM COMING THIS FAR DOWN THE MOUNTAIN BEFORE.
LUCKILY I WAS PREPARED FOR THIS PRECISE EVENTUALITY.
I NEED YOU TO TAKE THIS BELL, TWIG-
-AND TIE IT AROUND HIS NOSE. THAT WAY, IF HE BUDGES, WE'LL HEAR IT.
NOT THAT HE WILL...
..YOU KNOW, JUST IN CASE A CLOUD GOES OVER OR SOMETHING..

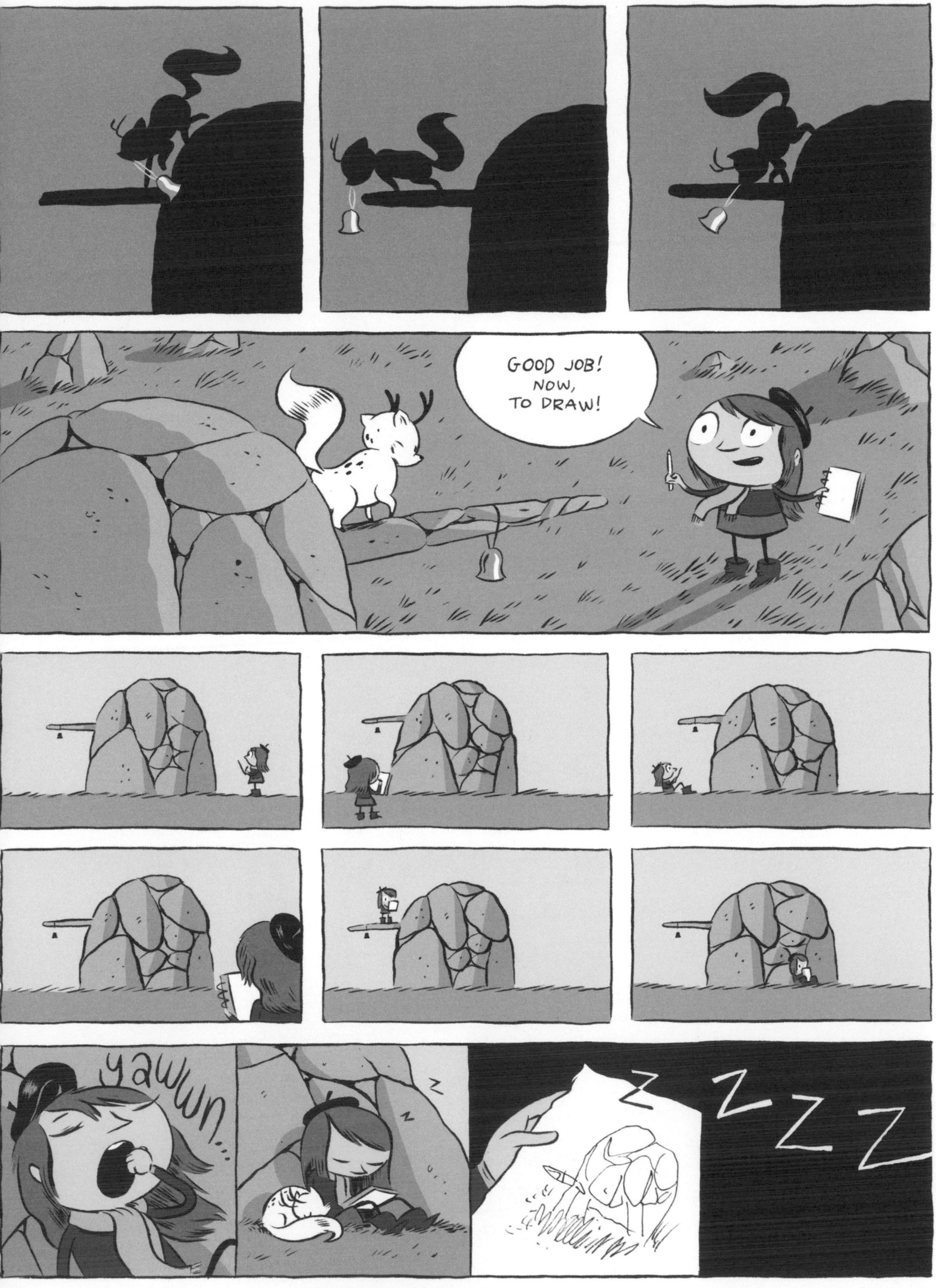
GOOD JOB! NOW, TO DRAW!
yawwn...
z
z
Z Z Z Z

[redacted]

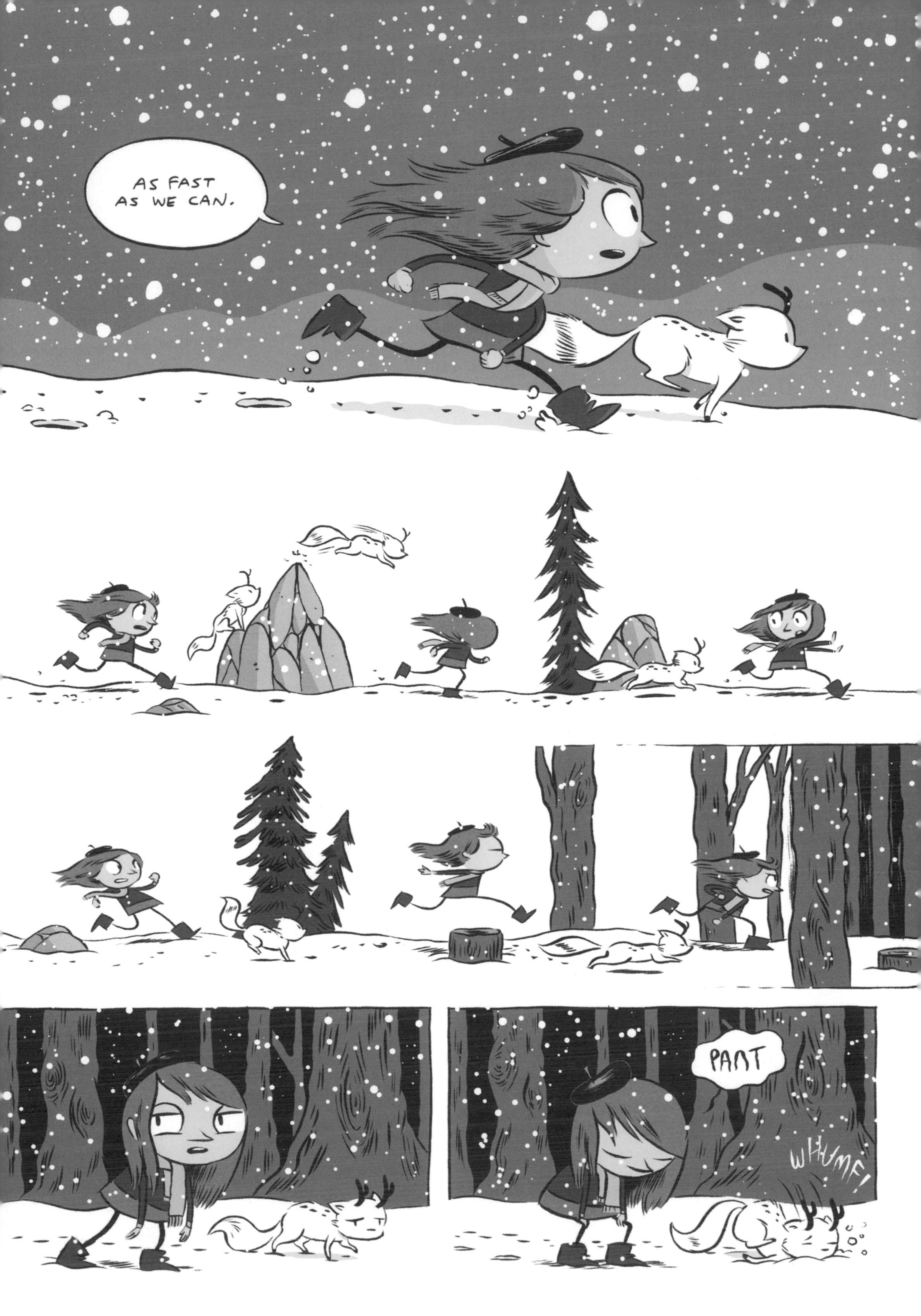
AS FAST AS WE CAN.
PANT
WHUMF!

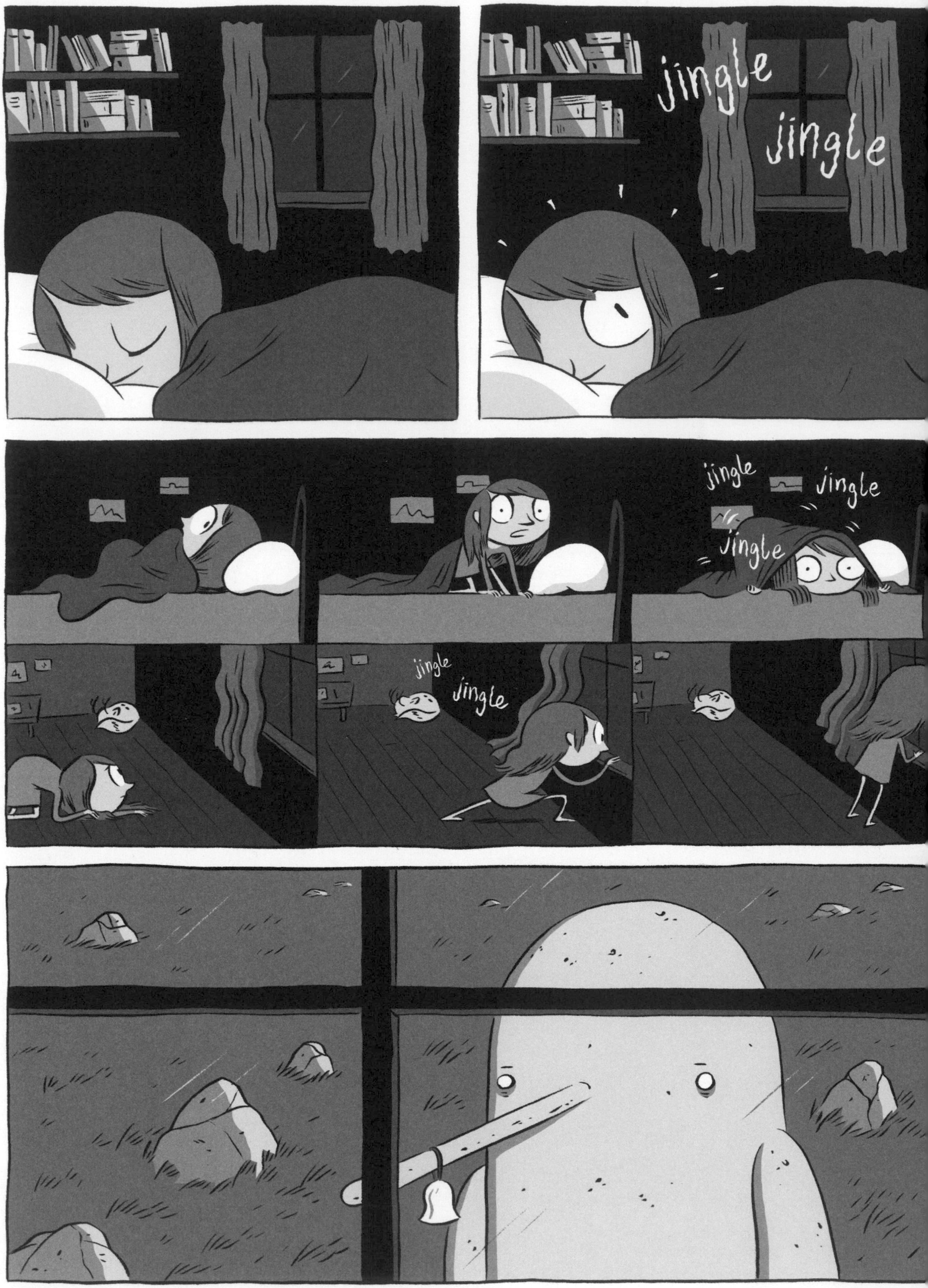
jingle
jingle
jingle
jingle
jingle
jingle
jingle

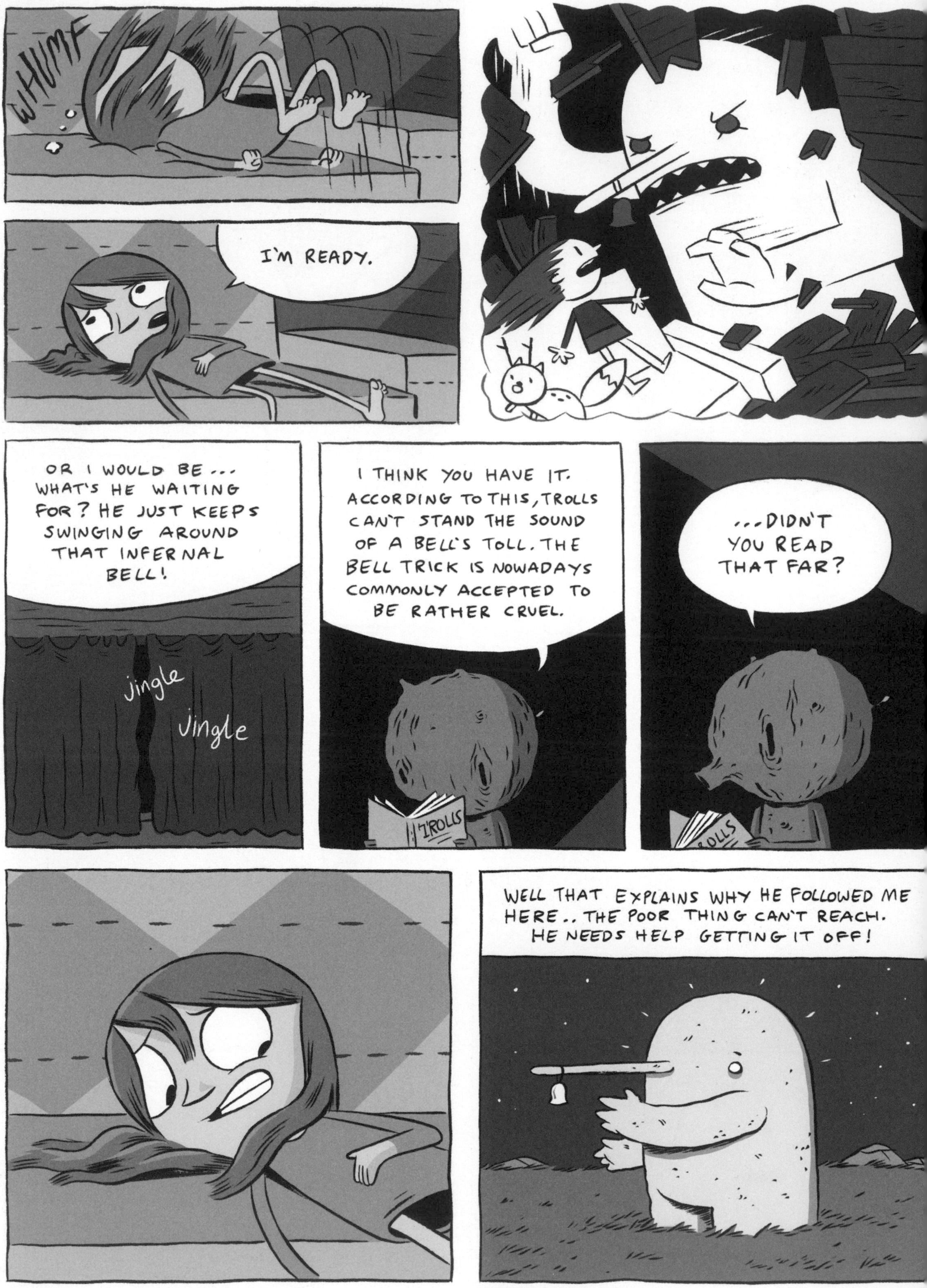
WHUMF
I'M READY.
OR I WOULD BE... WHAT'S HE WAITING FOR? HE JUST KEEPS SWINGING AROUND THAT INFERNAL BELL!
jingle
jingle
I THINK YOU HAVE IT. ACCORDING TO THIS, TROLLS CAN'T STAND THE SOUND OF A BELL'S TOLL. THE BELL TRICK IS NOWADAYS COMMONLY ACCEPTED TO BE RATHER CRUEL.
TROLLS
...DIDN'T YOU READ THAT FAR?
TROLLS
WELL THAT EXPLAINS WHY HE FOLLOWED ME HERE.. THE POOR THING CAN'T REACH. HE NEEDS HELP GETTING IT OFF!

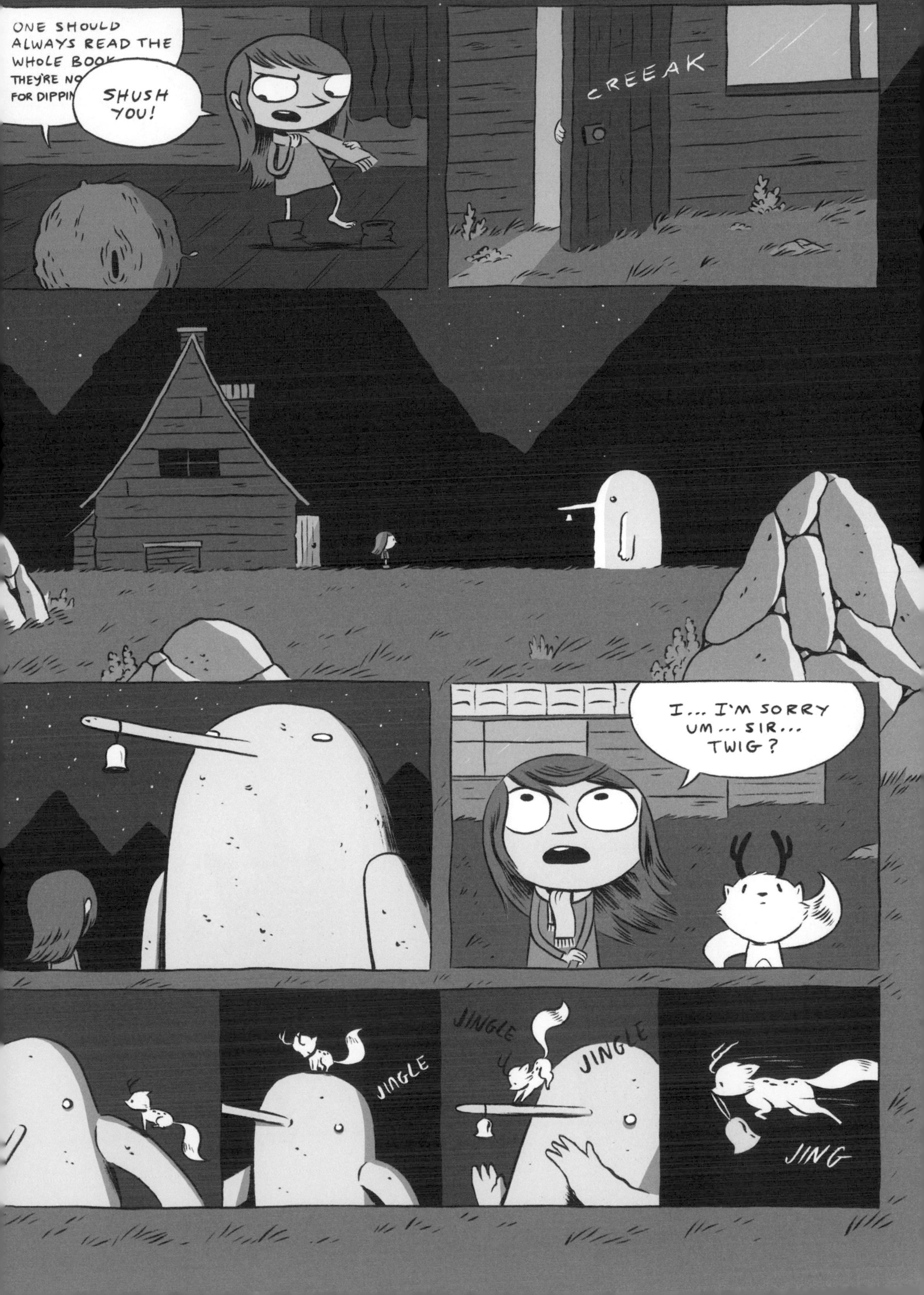
ONE SHOULD ALWAYS READ THE WHOLE BOOK
THEY'RE NO
FOR DIPPIN
SHUSH YOU!
CREEAK
I... I'M SORRY UM... SIR... TWIG?
JINGLE
JINGLE
JINGLE
JING

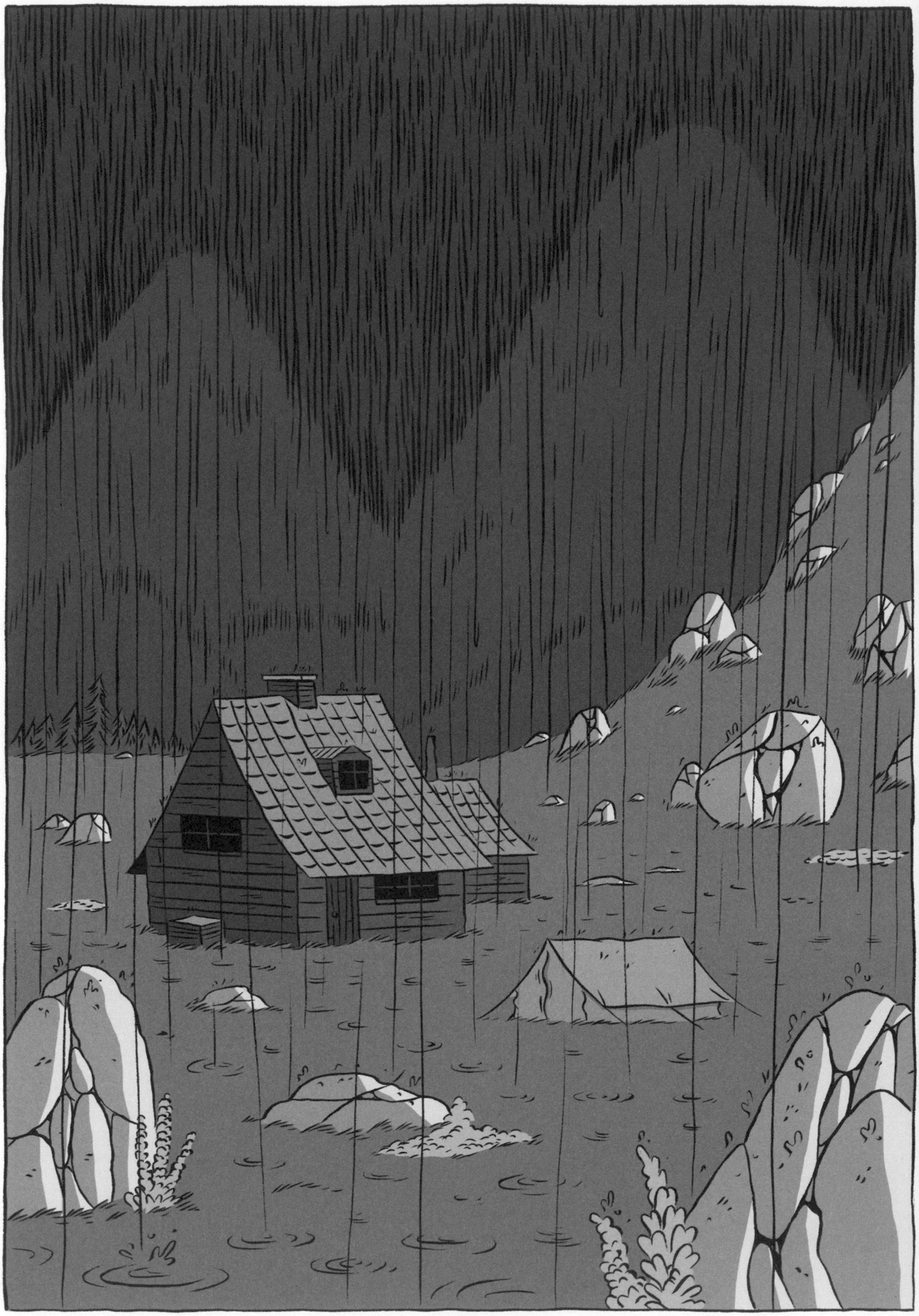

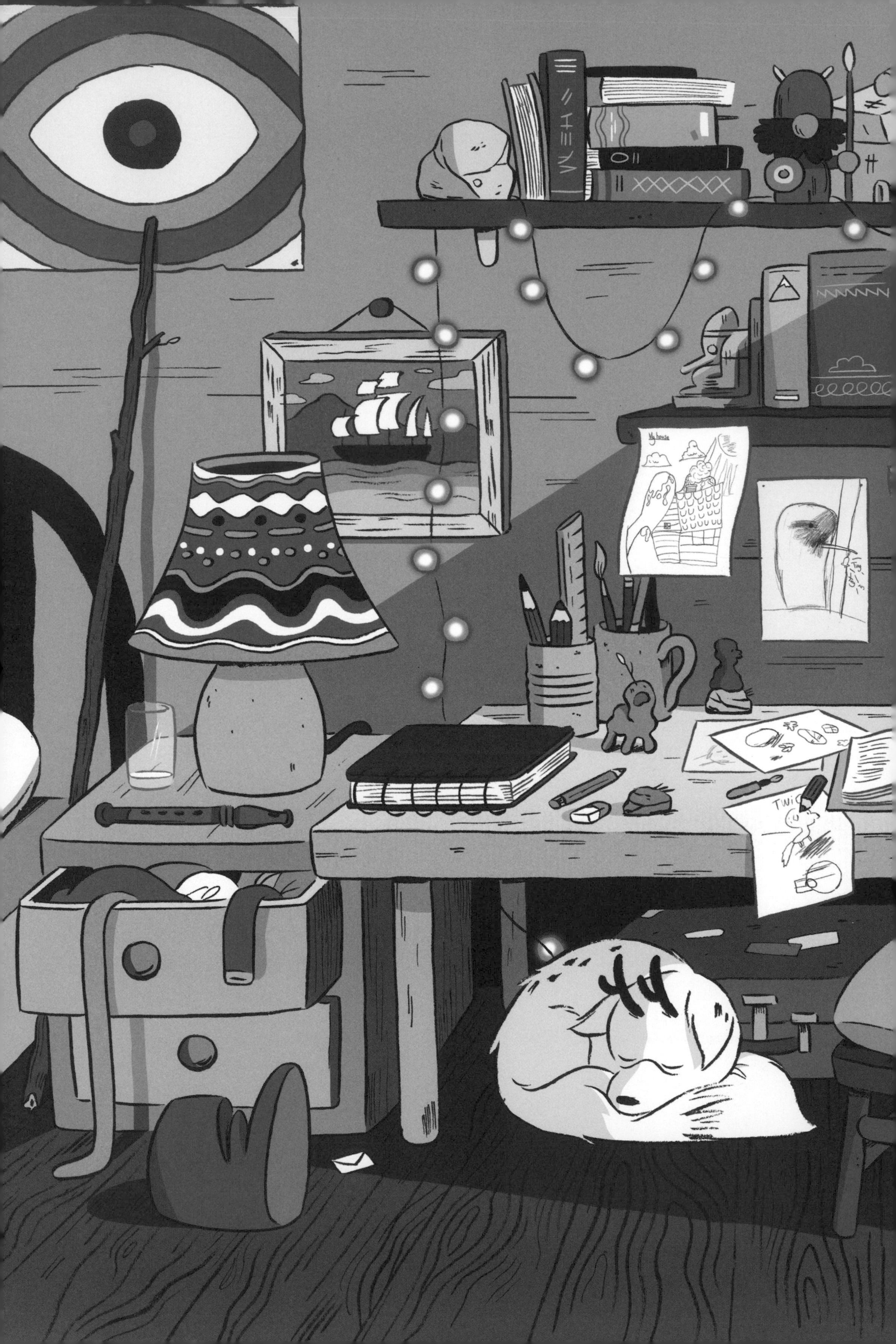
My house
Ting

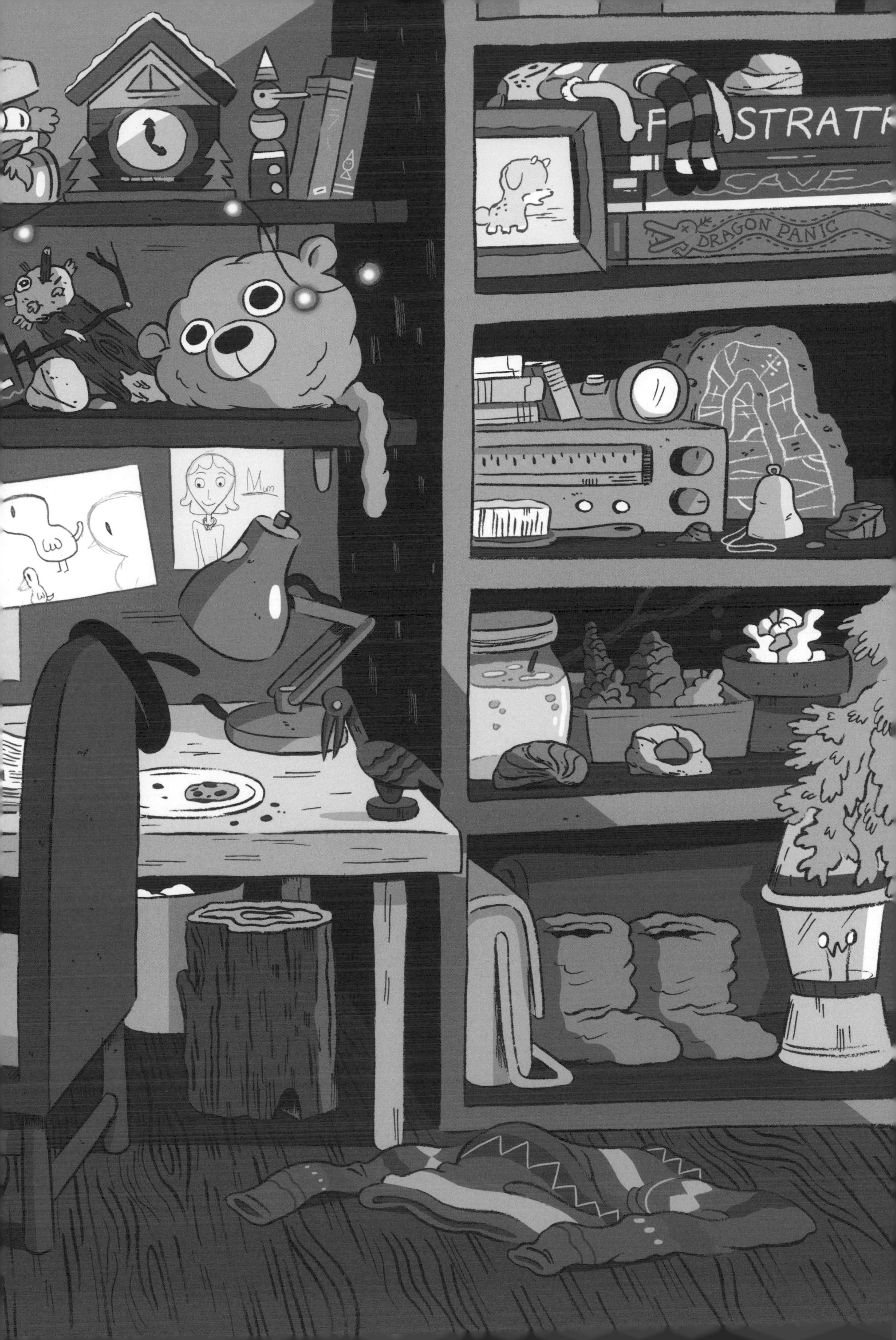
Mum
CAVE
DRAGON PANIC

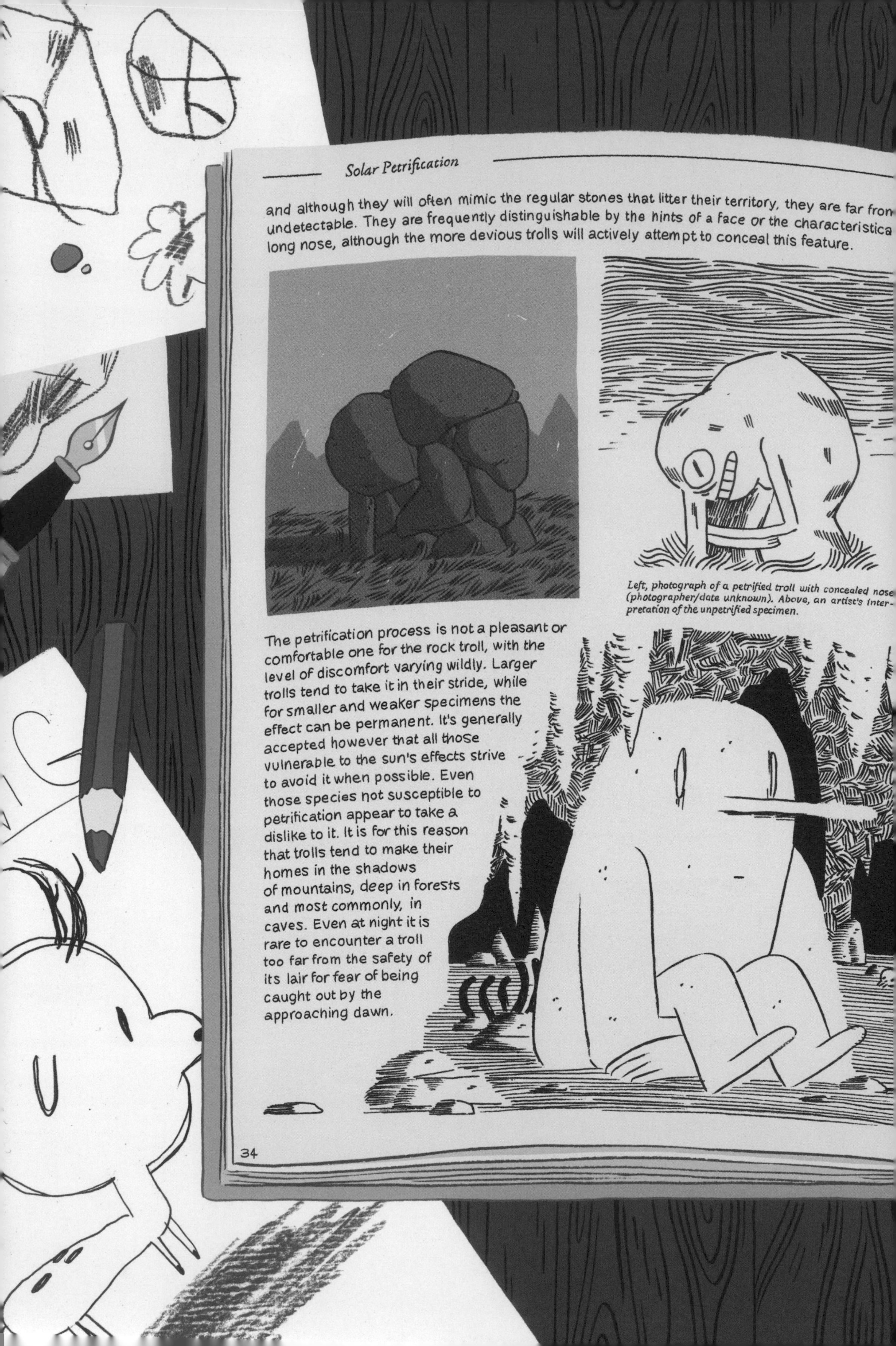
Solar Petrification
and although they will often mimic the regular stones that litter their territory, they are far from undetectable. They are frequently distinguishable by the hints of a face or the characteristica long nose, although the more devious trolls will actively attempt to conceal this feature.
Left, photograph of a petrified troll with concealed nose (photographer/date unknown). Above, an artist's interpretation of the unpetrified specimen.
The petrification process is not a pleasant or comfortable one for the rock troll, with the level of discomfort varying wildly. Larger trolls tend to take it in their stride, while for smaller and weaker specimens the effect can be permanent. It's generally accepted however that all those vulnerable to the sun's effects strive to avoid it when possible. Even those species not susceptible to petrification appear to take a dislike to it. It is for this reason that trolls tend to make their homes in the shadows of mountains, deep in forests and most commonly, in caves. Even at night it is rare to encounter a troll too far from the safety of its lair for fear of being caught out by the approaching dawn.
34

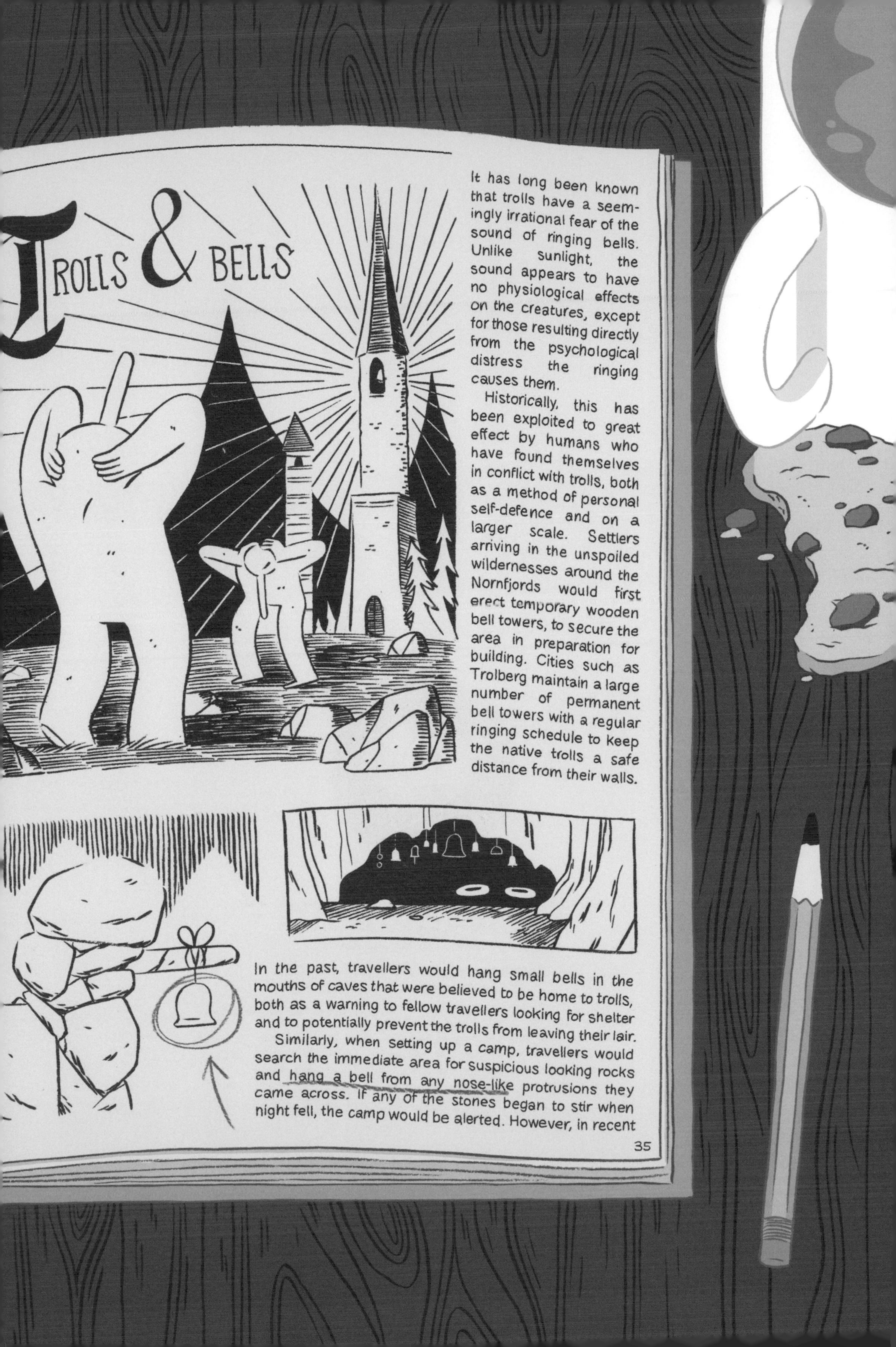

Trolls & Bells

It has long been known that trolls have a seemingly irrational fear of the sound of ringing bells. Unlike sunlight, the sound appears to have no physiological effects on the creatures, except for those resulting directly from the psychological distress the ringing causes them.

Historically, this has been exploited to great effect by humans who have found themselves in conflict with trolls, both as a method of personal self-defence and on a larger scale. Settlers arriving in the unspoiled wildernesses around the Nornfjords would first erect temporary wooden bell towers, to secure the area in preparation for building. Cities such as Trolberg maintain a large number of permanent bell towers with a regular ringing schedule to keep the native trolls a safe distance from their walls.

In the past, travellers would hang small bells in the mouths of caves that were believed to be home to trolls, both as a warning to fellow travellers looking for shelter and to potentially prevent the trolls from leaving their lair.

Similarly, when setting up a camp, travellers would search the immediate area for suspicious looking rocks and hang a bell from any nose-like protrusions they came across. If any of the stones began to stir when night fell, the camp would be alerted. However, in recent

THANKS TO PHILIPPA, MY FAMILY, MARTHA, JULES AND EVERYBODY AT NOBROW.

ORIGINALLY APPEARING IN PRINT IN 2010 AS HILDAFOLK.
© 2010 NOBROW LTD. AND LUKE PEARSON.

HILDA AND THE TROLL IS © 2013 FLYING EYE BOOKS.
THIS IS A THIRD EDITION PRINTED IN 2018.

ALL ARTWORK AND CHARACTERS WITHIN ARE © 2013 NOBROW LTD. AND LUKE PEARSON.

PUBLISHED BY FLYING EYE BOOKS, AN IMPRINT OF NOBROW LTD.
27 WESTGATE STREET, LONDON, E8 3RL

PRINTED IN POLAND ON FSC® CERTIFIED PAPER.

ISBN: 978-1-909263-14-7

ORDER FROM WWW.FLYINGEYEBOOKS.COM

HILDA'S DRAWINGS APPEARING ON PP. 32-35 BY MARTHA NORMAN.

JOIN THE ADVENTURES OF OUR FAVOURITE BLUE-HAIRED HEROINE IN THE WORLD OF HILDAFOLK!

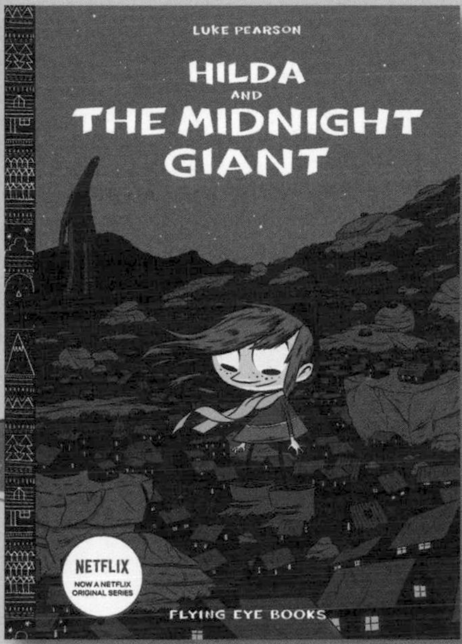
LUKE PEARSON
HILDA AND THE MIDNIGHT GIANT
NETFLIX
NOW A NETFLIX ORIGINAL SERIES
FLYING EYE BOOKS

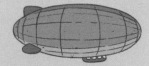

HILDA AND THE MIDNIGHT GIANT

HARDBACK ISBN 978-1-909263-17-8
PAPERBACK ISBN 978-1-909263-79-6

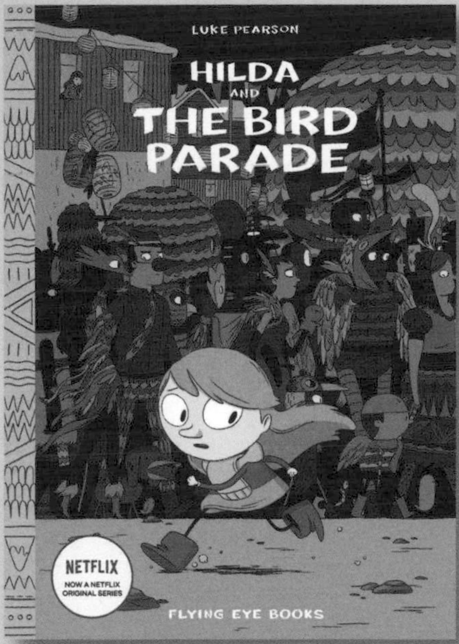
LUKE PEARSON
HILDA AND THE BIRD PARADE
NETFLIX
NOW A NETFLIX ORIGINAL SERIES
FLYING EYE BOOKS

HILDA AND THE BIRD PARADE

HARDBACK ISBN 978-1-909263-06-2
PAPERBACK ISBN 978-1-911171-02-7

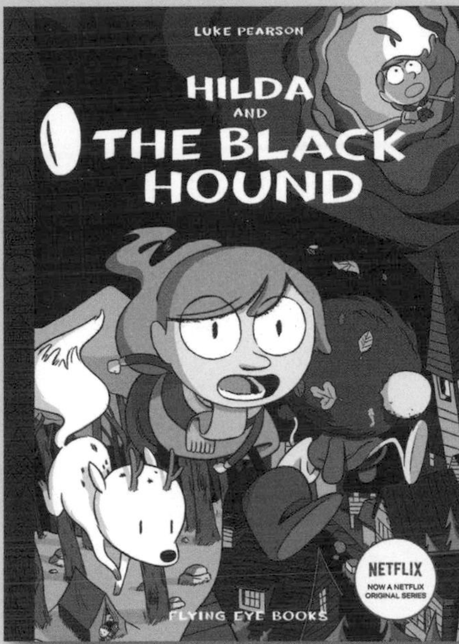
LUKE PEARSON
HILDA AND THE BLACK HOUND
NETFLIX
NOW A NETFLIX ORIGINAL SERIES
FLYING EYE BOOKS

HILDA AND THE BLACK HOUND

HARDBACK ISBN 978-1-909263-18-5
PAPERBACK 978-1-911171-07-2

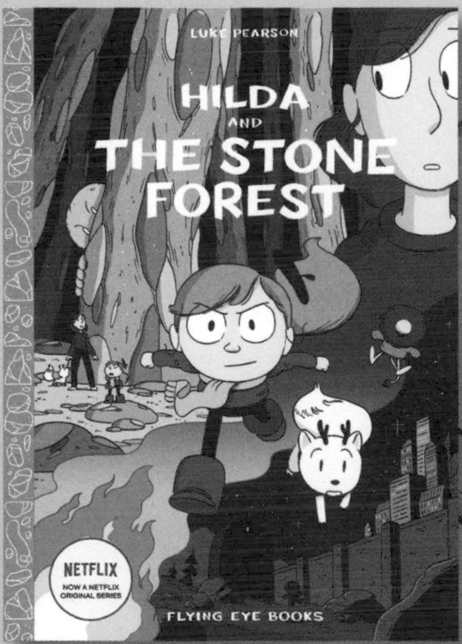
LUKE PEARSON
HILDA AND THE STONE FOREST
NETFLIX
NOW A NETFLIX ORIGINAL SERIES
FLYING EYE BOOKS

HILDA AND THE STONE FOREST

HARDBACK ISBN 978-1-909263-74-1
PAPERBACK ISBN 978-1-911171-71-3

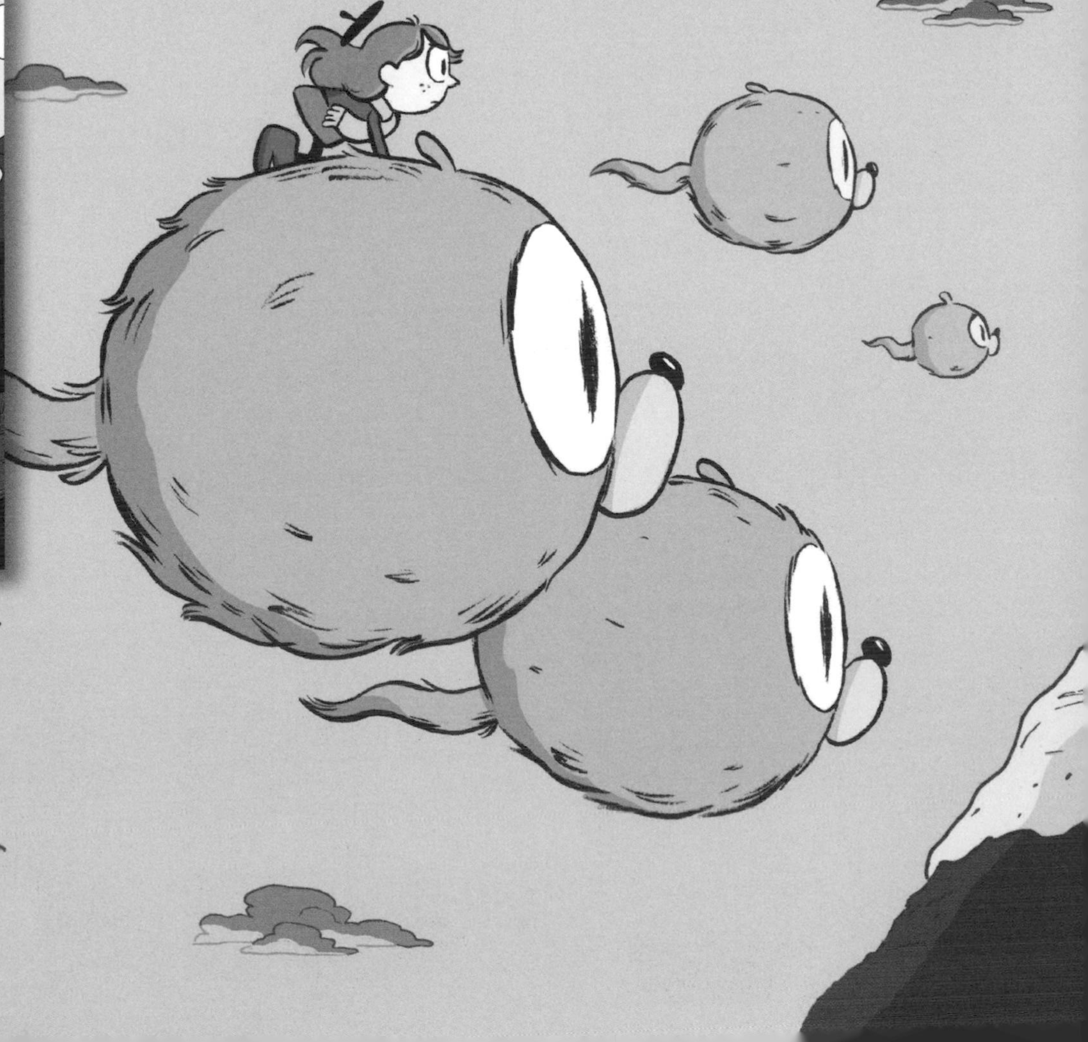

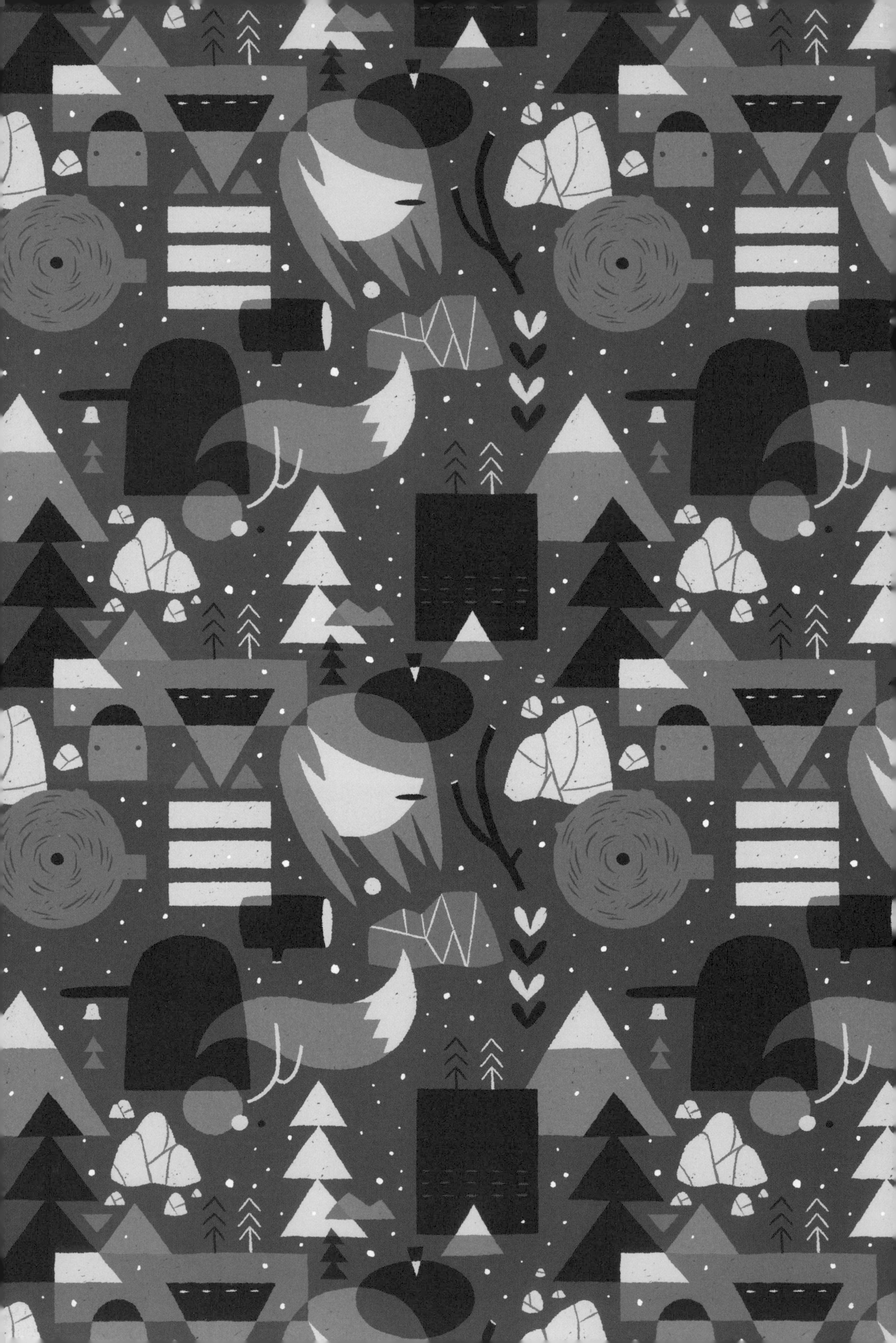